THIS BOOK BELONGS TO:

....

....

....

For all the little BEASTIES,
and especially for Will.

ORCHARD BOOKS
First published in Great Britain in 2021 by The Watts Publishing Group
2 4 6 8 10 9 7 5 3 1 • Text and Illustrations © Matt Robertson, 2021
The moral rights of the author/illustrator have been asserted. All rights reserved.
A CIP catalogue record for this book is available from the British Library.

HB ISBN 978 1 40835 160 4 • PB ISBN 978 1 40835 161 1
Printed and bound in China

MIX
Paper from
responsible sources
FSC
www.fsc.org
FSC® C104740

Orchard Books, an imprint of Hachette Children's Group
Part of The Watts Publishing Group Limited
Carmelite House, 50 Victoria Embankment, London EC4Y 0DZ
An Hachette UK Company • www.hachette.co.uk • www.hachettechildrens.co.uk

Matt Robertson

Boo, Little BEASTIE!

ORCHARD

Bertie Beastie was a happy little beast.
He liked dancing the BEASTLY BOP...

splashing in the
STINKY SWAMP...

practising his
BEASTLY ROAR...

and SLURPING
**SLIPPERY, SLIMY
SLUGS** for his tea.

But there was one thing that sometimes made Bertie feel sad . . .

He didn't have any friends to play his beastly games with.

Bertie tried playing snap with the swamp crocodiles, but they didn't understand the rules.

Ping-pong was no fun for just one . . .

and when he tried to play hide-and-shriek, no one came to find him.

Poor Bertie
was tired of being
ALL ALONE.

Then one day Bertie spotted something ...
"Wow – the Big City looks like lots of BEASTLY FUN.
Maybe I'll find some friends there!"
So off he went, and in no time at all ...

PUMPKIN FUN

SPOOKY FUN

BOO!

he made it to the hustling, bustling city. With an excited growl, Bertie set off to find some new friends.

Welcome to THE BIG CITY

First Bertie tried the park. He raised a hairy paw and waved.

"Hi! I'm Bertie. Will you be my friend?"

"EEEEEEEEEEK!

A BEAST!"

Then he tried the library. He smiled his toothiest smile and said . . .

"Hello! I'm Bertie!"

"HEEEEEEEELP! A BEEEEEEAST!"

Bertie searched the whole city, but wherever he went, everyone just screamed and ran away.

MUSEUM

AAAAAAARRGH!

"Why are they all afraid of me?" Bertie wondered. "I just wanted to find some **BEASTLY FRIENDS** to play with."

Darkness began to fall and spooky shadows crept in. Bertie had never felt so lonely.

But just then . . . he saw some strange lights bobbing towards him.

LANTERNS!

Carried by . . .

LITTLE BEASTIES!

"Hi, I'm Bertie. Can I play with you?"

"Of course!" said one little beastie.

"Great costume!" said another.

"Costume? What costume?"
muttered Bertie.
But no one heard him.

Bertie and the little beasties **SPOOKED** and **STOMPED.**

They **HOWLED**

and **ROARED**

from house to house.

Bertie had never had so much fun! Though he wasn't sure why they kept shouting . . .

"TRICK OR TREAT!"

"It's your turn next, Bertie," whispered one little beastie.

Bertie took a deep breath . . .

. . . and let out his most
MONSTROUS
ROAR!

TRICK OR TRE

WELCOME

The little beasties had
never heard a roar **SO FIERCE**.
They looked at Bertie a little more closely . . .

They had never
seen claws
SO SHARP...

or teeth
SO POINTY...

or fur SO SCRUFFY.

"HANG ON,
ARE YOU...

"...A REAL BEAST?!"

Bertie started to cry.
"Please don't run away. I've
always wanted friends like you."

"Run away?" said the little beasties. "But we think you're . . .

"ROARSOME!!!

Can you teach us to be BEASTLY, just like you?"

"Of course I can!" said Bertie.

At last, Bertie had some friends!

When the little beasties came to play,
Bertie taught them how to dance the
BEASTLY BOP...

splash in the STINKY SWAMP…

and practise their
BEASTLY ROARS!
But when teatime came around …

"EWWWWW! We're not eating those!"

"All the more for ME!" said Bertie, with a BIG, BEASTLY
SLUUUURRRRRP!